W9-CFA-615

CHIPMUNKS
ON THE DOORSTEP

CHIPMUNKS
ON THE DOORSTEP

written and illustrated by

EDWIN TUNIS

THOMAS Y. CROWELL COMPANY *New York*

Books by Edwin Tunis

CHIPMUNKS ON THE DOORSTEP

THE YOUNG UNITED STATES

SHAW'S FORTUNE

COLONIAL CRAFTSMEN

FRONTIER LIVING

INDIANS

COLONIAL LIVING

WHEELS

WEAPONS

OARS, SAILS AND STEAM

Typography by Jack Jaget

MANUFACTURED IN THE UNITED STATES OF AMERICA

L. C. Card 73-132305

ISBN 0-690-19044-1
0-690-19045-X (LB)

1   2   3   4   5   6   7   8   9   10

ACKNOWLEDGMENTS

Since the author is no scientist, help and guidance has been needed and was generously given by such "ordained scholars" as Fred E. Barkalow, Jr., Professor of Zoology and Forestry, North Carolina State University at Raleigh; John L. Paradiso, Systematic Zoologist, Fish and Wildlife Service, United States Department of the Interior; and Paul Voorhis, Linguist, Department of Anthropology, Smithsonian Institution. I thank them. The able help of librarians is indispensable. I thank those of the Enoch Pratt Free Library in Baltimore and of The Welsh Medical Library of Johns Hopkins University for giving it patiently and cheerfully.

My wife, Elizabeth, comes near to being a collaborator. Many of her observations and experiences are incorporated in the text, and we have discussed almost every statement in it to the advantage, we hope, of clarity and accuracy.

E. T.

Long Last

 FOREWORD

This is a book about an animal of little economic importance. His body is edible but too small to bother with except in dire emergency. His fur is soft and attractively patterned, but the hair is short and the pelt is so small that joining a number of them into a garment is a tedious job. He does some good and little if any harm either to nature or to the works of man. Once in a while he sinks a burrow so close to a house that it leads water into the cellar. In the days when reforestation was done by direct seeding, foresters railed against the chipmunk because he dug up the seeds. When they found that the planting of selected nursery seedlings produced better trees, they took Chippy off their blacklist; he had no interest in young trees.

It is his personality that recommends him. Long ago, someone writing in *The New York Times* expressed it well: the chipmunk is "graceful without being vain, well dressed without being showy, friendly without being intrusive. [He is] fun-loving without being silly, wise without being assertive, cautious without being afraid—and all over the scene without being a bore." Some of that can be applied to the gray squirrel, but he is an insistent lummox and sometimes, with no provocation, he bites. Chippy's charm makes him easy to watch, and he makes himself easy to see. These are the reasons for this book.

This is not a story. It is the straight truth so far as the author can determine it, but it is not a scientific treatise, either. All of the scientific terms in it are corralled in two paragraphs. This is not to say that the book has no solid basis. In addition to many in other publications, the articles that deal with the genus *Tamias* in the *Journal of Mammalogy* and the *Zoological Record* have been examined. Some of these that inquire closely into the interior machinery of the small beast have been skipped.

CHIPMUNKS
ON THE DOORSTEP

I<small>T IS A QUIET PLACE.</small> Our small house sits in an irregular partially cleared space within the edge of a thick woods that in thirty years has come to tolerate the intrusion. Tall tulip "poplars," black oaks, hickory, and a scattering of other large trees are interspersed with a lower growth of dogwood and shadblow. Up until about 1915 this was part of a great chestnut forest; the district is still called Chestnut Ridge. But blight wiped out the trees along with the rest of their kind in the eastern United States. Even the stumps are gone now, but their last remnants showed that they once supported trunks six feet thick.

The land here slopes gently southeastward into a shallow valley, largely cleared, in which a minuscule stream rises from a springhead. Beyond the valley, a succession of low hills are separated by similar valleys. The nearest dwelling is a city block away. It is almost that far by a crooked lane to the highway, not a heavily traveled one since it goes nowhere in particular.

We had originally intended to have a dog and a cat or two, but they would certainly have distressed the birds and beasts that already lived here and these proved so endlessly entertaining that domestic pets went by the board. Besides, squirrels, cottontails, and woodpeckers scarcely notice when those odd bipeds leave the place, and they never require boarding in a kennel, or any care from a veterinarian. None of these natives is unusual; they are all the common inhabitants of woodlands in the Middle Atlantic states. The occasional deer are the most spectacular of them, and certainly not the least beautiful. They wander through in twos and threes and only in winter group to form what may by courtesy be called a herd; eight or ten together are as many as anyone here has seen. But though they live in the back reaches of the same large wood of which ours is a small part, and though they come into the open at dawn and dusk to feed on our neighbor's young grain, the deer are accidental visitors that try to keep out of the sight of men and usually leave with speed and breath-stopping grace as soon as they spot one.

The animal that from the first fascinated us, and that has continued to interest us most, is about the same general color as a deer and in his way quite as graceful, but his three ounces are less than a five-hundredth of a deer's weight. This of course is the chipmunk, familiarly spoken of and to as "Chippy." He is so insignificantly small that his whole body would hardly make a mouthful. He has therefore never interested hunters, and so, more than any other fur-bearer in these parts, he tolerates the company of humans and even seems to seek it.

When we eat lunch on the terrace, a bowl of peanuts for chipmunks stands on the table and there are nearly always customers for them. They are just common supermarket peanuts, roasted in the shell. One old friend has a hole between the stones of the terrace itself; another lives a couple of feet from the edge, in the periwinkle that covers the woods floor. Others, from both ends of the house and even from the front of it, hear voices and arrive expectant. Most of these outlanders wait ten feet off for a nut to be tossed their way. Members of the inner circle stand upon no ceremony; they mount to the table top by way of a chair and help themselves.

All isn't entirely peaceful. The terrace residents claim the area as theirs and use up a lot of time and energy driving trespassers back into their own yards. Once in a while two customers meet on the table. They glower for a long moment. Then some mysterious telepathy triggers action in both at the same instant and the chase starts. Crockery and glass sometimes suffer small accidents. One or the other

of the opponents always dominates. It seems that both know from the start which will flee and which will pursue.

The chipmunk population is densest near the house. It thins out gradually in the woods beyond until the residences of the "wild" chipmunks, as we usually speak of them, are quite widely separated. There are parts of the woods which, as Ernest Thompson Seton noticed in Canada, appear to harbor no chipmunks at all, though to humans one part looks as habitable as another. On the face of things, the clustering around the house would seem to be due to the handouts that come from it. Yet some chips that live in the immediate "suburbs" and circulate freely in the clearing get nuts only when they chance upon one that was somehow missed. Worrying friends warn us that our population explosion will undermine the house. But a check made just now with a spirit level shows that it still stands true after thirty years.

The names of the chipmunk

John Josselyn, a seventeenth-century English traveler, called Chippy a "mouse squirrel" but the name was several sizes too small. One of the names the English colonists gave him was "hackee," or "hackie." Dictionaries say this is "echoic of the animal's call." Probably there is something to this because they also called him a "hacking squirrel," but among the noises he makes none sounds much like "hack" to a modern ear. Audubon used "hackee," so it was still current in the early 1800's.

The earliest form of the word "chipmunk" was "chitmuk"; English dictionaries still spell it "chipmuck." Back in 1896, A. F. Chamberlain produced an explanation of the origin of "chitmuk." The Chippewa word *achitaumo* (squirrel) was pronounced by the Indians with a glottal click on the final "o." These clicks occur in most Indian languages and readily suggest a "k" sound to a speaker of English. Pass "achitamok" from one Yankee to another several times, and it could hardly miss being pared down to "chitmuk." Oddly, the settlers probably picked the wrong word. The Chippewas had another, *agwingoss*, meaning small squirrel, which would fit the purpose better.

Henry W. Longfellow, along with others, spelled *achitaumo* as *adjidaumo* and said, in his *Hiawatha*, that it meant "tail in air." But

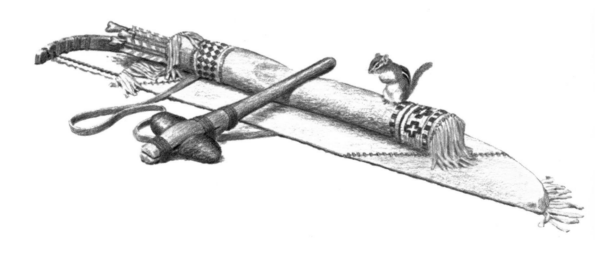

achit- meant "head down" and the name almost certainly referred to the way squirrels come down a tree. The Chippewas lived around the western Great Lakes, so they knew a variety slightly different from the East Coast chipmunks. The Lenape (Delaware) Indians, who lived in lower New York and eastern Pennsylvania, probably called our Chippy *haniqus*. Since this word also meant "mouse," it may hint at the origin of Josselyn's "mouse squirrel."

Chippy does belong to the squirrel family that is distributed through all of the continents except Australia. Squirrels in turn belong to the order of rodents. In 1758, the Swedish botanist Linnaeus, who seems to have provided scientific names for most of the plants and animals of eastern North America, assumed that Chippy was simply a squirrel with stripes and called him *Sciurus striatus* accordingly. In 1811, Gustav Illiger put the chipmunk into a separate genus (still within the squirrel family). On the strength of his habits and certain distinctive characteristics of his skull, Illiger renamed him *Tamias* (a steward, one who stores provisions) *striatus* (striped). *Tamias* indicates the genus, *striatus* the species. Later zoologists have further divided the species into several subspecies, chiefly on the basis of color variations. The chipmunks of the West differ greatly from the eastern ones. They are Asiatic chipmunks, belonging to the genus *Eutamias*, which apparently came to America along with, or perhaps ahead of, the Indians over the land bridge that once crossed the Bering Sea; or maybe they went the other way, as the horse did. *Eutamias* is somewhat smaller than *Tamias* and a bit grayer. One species of *Eutamias* lives far enough east to mix with the eastern variety around the western Great Lakes. This one is the smallest known chipmunk. Together, the two genera account for all the chipmunks in the world; there are none in Europe, Africa, or South America.

Let's not worry here about small variations; a casual glance hardly notices them. What we discover about our particular Chippy will apply to all of his eastern cousins. These live from Florida as far up into Canada as the forests reach, and from the Atlantic Ocean as far west as Oklahoma, though this should not be taken to mean that they are found in all states that far west. Perhaps we should note that the

5

Invader

particular subspecies that comes under our eye is *Tamias striatus fisheri*. The last word of his name does not indicate any preference for fish; it is made from the name of the man who described his differences from other subspecies. *Tamias striatus fisheri* lives in the Middle Atlantic states, from the lower Hudson River valley to southern Virginia, and as far west as Ohio.

Shape and color

Male chipmunks are slightly smaller than females. A female is just about nine inches long overall. That sounds larger than she looks because nearly four inches of her length is tail. A chippy's head is conical, with quite large bright eyes that look black because they are all pupil, showing no iris at all. The ears, quite high on the head, are small and round. Of all animals probably a monkey's are the only ones shaped so nearly like human ears. Chippy's slender forepaws have four distinct "fingers" and a kind of thumb that seems to be a useless afterthought. Though he travels on four feet, Chippy constantly sits up and makes great use of his forepaws as hands. It's likely that this is one of the characteristics that endear him to humans. A chip eating a nut or a large grape held between his forepaws is an engaging sight. Unless you see him do this from the side, at eye level, you are unlikely to see his mouth at all. He has no visible chin and the small pink opening of his mouth hides under, and well behind, his nose.

6

Chippy's "arms" are quite short and are correspondingly strong, as they have need to be, for he is a mighty digger. His somewhat longer hind legs are strong, too, as he proves by his jumping ability. Chip makes nothing of a standing vertical leap from the ground to the arm of a chair. A man, leaping proportionately, could jump to the eaves of a two-story house. Once, a chipmunk here possessed himself of a black walnut still in its husk and far too large to be held in his mouth. He hugged it to his chest with both forepaws and proceeded home in a series of prodigious kangaroo hops.

A chipmunk's hind feet, an inch and a half long from toe to heel, are quite visible when he is in motion, but he hides them under him when he crouches at rest and when he sits up. Actually his legs give him full support in these positions but since they are hidden his appearance suggests an egg balanced on its small end. The effect of insecurity is increased by the angular curve of his spine, which puts his head so far forward that he seems about to tip over forward.

A squirrel's tail lashes from side to side as it helps to maintain his balance on precarious perches in trees. A flying squirrel's tail is the rudder that steers his sweeping glides through the woods. A chipmunk may make some such uses of his tail at times but in the main it seems to serve only to express his emotions—and to warm his feet on cold days. Chippy, as indicated, is a rodent. It is perhaps unkind, but it is truthful to say that, if the hair were stripped from his tail, Chippy's shape would sadly resemble that of his disreputable cousin, the Norway rat. Happily, though some males lose an inch or so of tail, or occasionally almost all of it, in narrow escapes or in combats for prestige, most of the tails around here are decently furred.

A chipmunk's tail varies in appearance, depending on the angle from which it is viewed and on whether the fur on it lies flat, is slightly bristled, or stands straight out. Individual tail hairs are tawny near their roots and tan at their tips, with a short dark area between. When the hair lies flat, the tail looks solid gray; bristled, it is tawny with three dark stripes in it, one down the middle and two near the edges. The tail hairs are about half an inch long, so, even when his tail is fully expanded, Chippy wears no such plume as the one a gray squirrel flaunts.

right
forefoot

right
hind foot

actual size

7

Though his short fur is marked with strong patterns, Chippy is well camouflaged to blend with his normal background of dry leaves and sun-dappled shadow. His whole underside is creamy white and very showy but he keeps it hidden most of the time. The general color of his upper parts is brownish-tawny shading into tan on his feet and ears. In general he is near the color of a dry oak leaf. The brown color becomes quite ruddy on his rump and thighs. His pate, neck, and back are grayed by intermixed dark hairs which take over across his shoulders, making the fur there entirely gray.

Beginning just behind his shoulders and disappearing into the ruddy rump are five narrow dark stripes. One of them follows his backbone down the middle. The four outer stripes appear as two pairs, marking the boundary between back and sides. They are black, and each pair is separated by a cream-colored stripe so pale that it is commonly called white.

Remnants of the stripes appear on Chip's face. Light ones, bordered by dark, run from nose to ears above his eyes. Two more light stripes, below the eyes, have dark smudges under them. A dark streak runs from the rear corner of the eye to the ear. A black spot, right in the middle, appears just back of Chippy's nose.

There was a Cherokee legend about the back stripes: After man invented weapons and began to hunt, all the animals held a council and proposed that, in retaliation, each should inflict man with a disease. Only the chipmunk refused. Man didn't hunt him, he said, so he had no quarrel with man. This infuriated the other delegates and they at-

8

tacked Chippy. He fled and escaped, but not before the bear had raked him down the back with his claws. He still carries the marks. It was a remarkable bear that could come that near to catching a running chipmunk.

Grooming

Chippy is fastidious about the condition of his fur. He will suddenly interrupt what seems to be serious business and give himself a thorough grooming. He frequently moistens his forepaws with his tongue and shampoos his face, head, and ears. He performs this ablution at a speed the eye can barely follow, and a drawing can't even suggest. He has been known to pause on a human lap and go through this shampooing act before accepting a nut. Less often but several times a day at least, the toilette includes a thorough cleaning of the lower back and thighs. An area of the upper back and a space between the shoulders are out of reach and in summer a small parasitic fly rides there with complete

impunity. The final item in the cleanup is the tail. Chippy holds this with both hands and seems to comb the length of it with his teeth.

Chipmunks often pause to scratch themselves vigorously with a hind foot, and at times their grooming takes on an urgency that hints at the pursuit of fleas. Though this urgency is sometimes so great as to suggest that our chips have at least thirty-seven fleas each, a careful examination by Dr. J. S. Stanford of thirty-seven animals revealed only eleven fleas among the lot. Dr. Stanford also examined a chipmunk nest and found thirty fleas in it. Red mites also infest chipmunks now and then.

Isabel — two views of the same posture

Chestnuts

The built-in carrier

Chippy's distant cousin, the pocket gopher of the western plains (he is a rodent, but not a squirrel), gets his name from his cheek pouches. These are entirely outside the animal's mouth, and are lined with fur. Chippy has pouches made of his stretchable cheeks, which extend behind his jawbone well down onto his neck. He can get food into them only through his mouth, and they are lined with a mucous membrane like any other cheeks. To make access to the pouches easier, some of Chippy's teeth are left out, both above and below, between his long incisors in front and his grinders at the back. One may guess that the pouches developed at need because the dental arrangement was ready and waiting. Other squirrels, without pouches, have similar gaps in their dentures. Chippy stores winter food and often has to bring it home from considerable distances. For this he had to find a way to carry more than one nut at a time. The pouches solved the problem.

In the days when he could get them, Chippy could transport seven old-fashioned chestnuts on one trip, three in each cheek and one in his mouth. A full-grown chipmunk can pouch thirty corn kernels, but his limit on goobers is three, one in each side and one across the middle. He makes a frantic ado of getting a large peanut into a pouch. First he nips off the dried remnant of the stem, which apparently scratches the lining of his pouch, then, manipulating it feverishly with his paws, he tries it first in one side, then in the other. Finally, it is likely to go back

in the first side, where getting it into place may take much pushing and jaw working. What seems to be trial and failure is more probably purposeful moistening of the shell to allow the nut to slide comfortably into place. At times he confounds all this by shoving the first nut in with one quick gesture and looking up to ask for the next.

A few individuals will shell peanuts and pouch only the kernels. This easily triples carrying capacity. Those that start this way seem always to do it, unless they are startled during the shelling process. Those that start by carrying whole nuts seem never to learn the advantage of packing shelled ones. All hands are likely to eat any nut with a cracked shell on the spot. When a decent looking chipmunk stuffs both pouches full, he becomes a grotesque, but he doesn't know it. When his burden is peanuts in the shell, he rattles as he runs.

loading

loaded

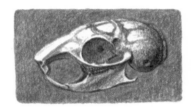

Teeth

More needs to be said about Chippy's teeth. His incisors are of such literally vital importance to him that he couldn't get his living without them, in fact cannot do so if any accident puts them out of commission. But this is true of all his cousins, from mice to beavers. He has four of these front teeth, two upper opposed to two lower. The upper ones serve mainly as holders, the lower pair do the biting and gnawing. Chippy's rear grinders just sit there like human teeth and are often worn down to the gums by the time he is through with them. If the hard-working incisors wore down in the same way, they would be gone long before he was through with them. Actually they do wear, but nature has compensated for it by making them continue to grow all through his life. She has also arranged to keep their cutting edges sharp by making the enamel on the rear surfaces slightly thinner than that on the front. Thus it wears away the least bit faster than the forward edges. A chipmunk, or any other squirrel, in captivity is likely to get softer food than he would find in nature. As a result his front teeth are not worn down fast enough to match growth. Unless they are artificially shortened, they will grow so long that the animal cannot eat.

In the wild, the incisors are long, curved, strong, yellow, and sharp. They can neatly nip off a berry, dissect a succulent bud, or chisel through the shell of a hickory nut. Most hickory nut shells are so hard that a hammer blow heavy enough to crack them is likely to crush the kernel inside. Chip's teeth are formidable weapons, too. Battling males scar one another permanently with them. Undoubtedly a well-placed bite on the spine could kill, but they don't seem to understand this;

no fight we have seen has resulted in a fatality. A chipmunk bite can be painful and even dangerous to a human, since it makes a deep puncture wound that certainly isn't sterile. But we have held them often on our hands, and had them nuzzle into a closed fist that held a nut, and have never yet been bitten. It is just luck that nothing has startled a nuzzler at the wrong moment.

Attitudes

When Chippy first wakes, especially on a damp, chilly morning, he is likely to mount his lookout and crouch miserably belly down like a

wet cat. When he does this in very early spring, he seems half-conscious, disregarding everything around him except whatever appears actually to threaten him. He will often take a similar crouching position in pleasant weather, but then it is more alert and he becomes a miniature imitation of the lions in front of the New York Public Library: five inches of preposterous dignity.

Usually, when he pauses in his explorations of the ground, he takes what is known around here as "the teapot position," sitting on his haunches with his forepaws hugging his chest. This is also the usual eating posture. He may wrap his tail around his hind feet, or just let it lie wherever it lands, but quite often he completes the picture by raising his tail in a double curve, like an italic S—providing the teapot with a handle.

Rhoda, the front yard chipmunk, so called because she lives under a rhododendron, will hold this position for ten minutes or more, al-

most motionless, but alert to every sound and smell that comes to her. If something (who knows what?) becomes really interesting, she will face the source of it and "stand up tall." Holding her sides with her forepaws, and pressing down with her tail for balance, she rises on the tips of her toes, straightens her hind legs and her back, and stretches her neck until her straining ears are an incredible eight inches (it looks more) from the ground. A similar but usually less extended stance serves for reaching berries and weed seeds.

Mousing around

Casual lope

Gaits

In his unending search for edible and storable food, Chippy gets over the ground by means of a variety of gaits. He can progress very slowly with a belly crawl which gives the effect of a stalking approach and sometimes actually is that. He can also walk as a horse walks, moving fore and hind feet on alternate sides, but he doesn't do much of this. Chippy never trots. For normal "mousing around" he uses a series of spurts with a gait that is actually repeated short jumps, giving the effect of a lope, interrupted by dead stops that may be short or long. When Chippy stops, he usually freezes completely. The length of the spurts varies, too, from a foot or so when inspecting, to ten or twelve feet when traveling. Only when startled, chased, or angry will a chipmunk move continuously with no pauses. Then he moves with real speed; a gray squirrel's fastest is a lumbering gallop compared with it. The eye cannot detect the leg action which accomplishes

Stalking

this speed; only a slow motion movie can do it. Yet two of the small animals here can move faster on short runs than Chippy can, the shrew and the vole. They are commonly seen, if at all, only as gray blurs.

The footprints Chippy leaves in mud show the difference in speed between a lope and a full run only by the gaps between the groups of prints. At the end of each jump, his front feet hit the ground first, close together, with one foot (usually the right) just a bit ahead of the other. His hind feet, hitting an instant later, leave their marks outside the front ones and somewhat ahead of them. Dr. Elsa Allen thinks that the longer the jumps the farther ahead the hind-foot tracks will be. To a casual glance, the fore and hind feet make similar impressions but there are noticeable distinctions. The forefeet make the narrower marks, show the imprint of but four toes, and often show a slight trailing mark behind the pad of the foot. The larger hind feet never make this but they do make five toe marks.

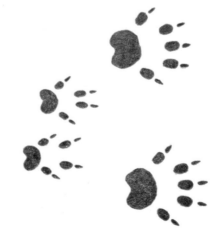

Tracks
(actual size)

Trails

When heading home, chipmunks seem to follow habitual trails that are deliberately circuitous, and they repeat a given route *exactly* the same way every time. For instance, one of them, whose front door is near one corner of a stone step in the garden, will pick up a peanut from a dish set in the grass, say, ten feet southwest of his home. He will move east, crossing the grass and the path, then travel north alongside the path, mount the step and run west across it, then dive south and down from its edge into his hole. He has traveled nearly thirty feet. Coming back for another nut he moves in a straight line from the hole to the original point of departure. He will repeat this pattern precisely, as long as nuts are available.

Another chip used to come to the terrace, from her home under a rock pile, by a dogleg route that was entirely reasonable. Returning she took to the woods, scurrying through the ground cover, passing around trees by running up them a couple of feet and coming down on the other side, and finally circling around to reach her rock pile from the rear. She repeated this whole cycle in every detail through a whole summer. The run up and around a tree trunk is a frequent maneuver, possibly intended to baffle the nose of a questing predator.

Climbing

Though the chipmunk spends almost all of his time on the ground or in it, he can also climb trees and often does so to get food, or merely because (apparently) he feels like climbing a tree. Like all squirrels, he clings to the bark with his claws, and descends head downward. He runs up a tree rapidly and with no noticeable effort but not quite so fast as a gray, a red, or a flying squirrel.

Chippy goes up oak trees and hickories for nuts, and up the tall tulip trees for their buds and blossoms that have some tasty part at their

base. Gray squirrels also like these, but they are clumsy about gathering them and drop enough to keep the chips fairly well supplied. Chippy likes dogwood blossoms, too. He pulls off the white bracts, one at a time, and stuffs them into his mouth with both hands. In the fall he returns to the dogwoods for their red berries. Once one fellow was far out on a twig, reaching for berries, when another chipmunk nipped him from behind. The nipped one lost his balance and only barely saved himself by grabbing the twig with his forepaws and hanging by them. He shrieked and kept on shrieking as he swung wildly back and forth, with his tail lashing in circles. The nipper watched him interestedly for a moment and then left to attend to more important matters. The victim presently managed to get his hind feet up to the twig, and hanging under it like a two-toed sloth, worked himself back to the branch from which the twig sprang. There he righted himself and headed for solid ground.

20

When Chip climbs a tree merely to get away from it all, he sits on a limb and lets the world below take care of itself. The limb may be ten feet up, or it may be fifty. Coming down, he often stops on the trunk a few feet from the ground and stretches, as other squirrels do, also. Keeping a firm grip on the bark with his spread hind feet, he lets go in front, puts his head back, arches his body away from the trunk, and stretches his forelegs out ahead of him.

Swimming

Chippy can swim quite well though he seldom does it voluntarily. There is an oblong goldfish pool here into which drinking or merely curious chipmunks fall now and then. The water is almost up to ground level, so they easily climb out again. Just once we saw a chipmunk come upon one end of the pool suddenly, and, unable to stop, dive in. He swam to the other end, climbed out, and shook himself inefficiently; then he groomed himself all over. Incidentally, Chippy is light enough to run across water lily pads almost "dry-shod."

One chipmunk that escaped from Dr. Allen fell into a pond and swam eight feet across a little cove; he landed running and vanished. Dr. Allen mentions a Mr. McIlvaine who saw a chipmunk jump into a lake deliberately and strike out for the opposite shore. Pursued with a boat, Chippy climbed onto a proffered oar, groomed himself—and jumped overboard again!

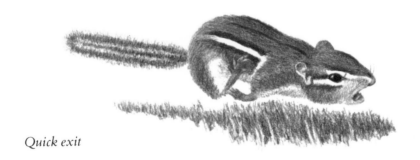

Quick exit

Senses

The brightness of a chipmunk's eyes results from their shiny blackness; it doesn't indicate keen vision. A hunt for a professional study on Chippy's eyes has drawn a blank, but even casual observation indicates that his eyesight is poor. Chippy hears a tossed nut hit the ground and runs toward it at once but he seldom runs *to* it. He stops somewhere in its vicinity and makes short circling casts until his nose tells him where

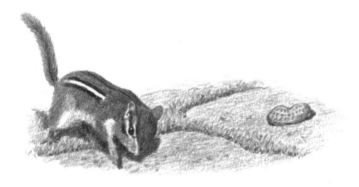

the nut is. He can do this as effectively in the thick four-inch-high ground cover as on mown grass or stone pavement. A chip taking a nut from your fingers will come right up to it, because he is used to doing it, or because he hears the kernel rattle in the shell. But once there, he seems to meet a confusion of smells and a similarity of shapes and perhaps colors; he often can't distinguish peanut from finger. His solution is to test the nearest object gently with his teeth. Sometimes he hits the nut on the first try; more often he samples a couple of fingers first.

Testing

On the other hand, with practice, he can neatly field a nut thrown directly to him. It seems probable that, like a frog, he can readily detect motion but not much else. Like all other modern animals, he quickly learns to disregard the noises of machinery. He will ignore a lawn mower, a passing airplane, or even the clatter of a low-flying helicopter—unless the moving shadow passes over him. When that happens, he vanishes like a blown-out candle flame.

Obviously Chippy's sense of smell is superb. He may not know that a nut shell is empty until he picks it up, but one sniff at a mushroom tells him whether it is good to eat or not. Quite often we watch a

Listening

chipmunk smell his way to the exact spot from which a nut has recently been removed. His hearing is as good as a dog's. The sound of another chipmunk barking far across the valley will alert him immediately and he will listen to it with concentrated interest. Often this sound is too faint for us to hear without cupping our ears with our hands.

A few "cat whiskers," short, dark, and visible only upon close examination, project from Chippy's upper lip. They certainly serve his perception in some way, but one can only guess at how. It is much the same with his sense of taste. Little can be said of it except that it must be there since Chippy rejects some foods that other animals like. Oddly enough, one of them is peanut butter and another is shelled pecans. Chipmunks are elsewhere recorded as liking shelled pecans, however. Birds are extremely fond of sweet cookies, as long as they are not spiced; all of our chipmunks investigate them and disdain them, yet there are records of chipmunks addicted to cake. They are frequently seen to lick the mortar between the bricks of the house walls. Assuming that the attraction might be a faint saltiness, we put some table salt on a dish and baited it with nuts. No, thank you. They removed the nuts and disregarded the salt.

Vocalizing

What has been mentioned here as "barking" was once known as "hacking." Modern writers usually call it "chipping," which suggests its higher notes; its lower ones could well be called "chucking." Chippy's rendering strongly suggests the sound made by a drummer when he taps a wooden block. Natural human equipment can approximate it by placing the tongue against the roof of the mouth, creating a slight suction behind it, and then snapping the tongue downward. Something done with the muscles of the throat can alter the tone over a range of perhaps four notes. Chippy seems to exceed this range. The human imitation falls far below the real thing in volume of sound.

Naturalists designate this chipping-chucking as the "call" of the chipmunk, but none of them seems to have a satisfactory answer as to why Chippy does it. He barks most often crouching on his favorite lookout, though now and again he starts up wherever he happens to be, even high up on a tree limb. No matter where he barks, he throws himself into the production with energy. Each "chuck" jerks his whole body forward convulsively and twitches his tail. Often he repeats the sound for ten minutes or more in a fixed rhythm, from 50 "chucks" up to 130 to the minute.

Barking

Echoing bark

Though other chipmunks listen attentively to distant barking, the performance of a near neighbor arouses no interest beyond occasionally moving them to join it. The note they add may be the same as or different from that of the original barker, but the rate of repetition is almost always identical. Sometimes the sounds come in unison; more often two barkers will alternate. A chorus of three or more creates a small bedlam.

The first sound of an outlander's barking made a visible impact on young Lucy seated perhaps eight feet from us on the terrace. She merely listened for a moment or two, then, without dropping her forefeet to the flagstone, she started interjecting very small barks, practice echoes, at quite long and irregular intervals. The sounds she made were not much more than audible to us; and instead of the customary spasm of the whole body, each bark merely inflated her cheek pouches slightly. She did not open her mouth at all, and as far as we have detected, no chipmunk opens his mouth to bark.

Mr. R. W. Shufeldt, writing in *Country Life* in 1919, suggested that chipmunks live in a constant state of terror and that their barking is an "all's well" signal to others. We can't agree. It seems that an animal as terrified as this would hardly advertise his whereabouts so loudly even if he felt, for the moment, that all was well. Further, animals in constant terror would tend to be furtive, to creep out of hiding only with great care, and to show signs of fear in their actions. Not so the chipmunk. Though he flees at the mere hint of danger, he lives his life between such crises (usually false alarms) with careless abandon, right out in the open.

Almost any sudden or unexpected motion startles a chipmunk and causes him to let out a piercing shriek. As he dives for cover the hair on his tail bristles until it looks like a bottle brush. Near the house, cover is often the open end of a metal downspout. He can scramble a couple of feet up the inside, advertising his presence with the frantic scratching of his effort to stay there. If the startled chip is at any distance from the nearest hidey-hole, he follows his initial shriek with a series of staccato squeals, delivered rapidly as he runs. Combatant chipmunks squeal as they fight but these squeals are of longer duration and are given at irregular intervals. They suggest "Ouch!" and "Take that!"

A chipmunk fight doesn't last long but while it's on, there's action. It starts with the tense glowering and the chase, long or short, that are the formal moves. Real activity begins when the pursuer catches his quarry. No sports reporter could follow the blows. The pair look like at least four as brown bodies tumble on the ground, seeking advantage and now and then getting it. Eeek! Round and round, over and

Battle

The winner

over. One gladiator will sometimes pop out of the scramble in a back flip that exposes his gleaming belly to the sky. For all the vehemence, we have never seen a loser unable to run away from a fight he had lost, nor have we ever discovered how he knew he was licked. The victor, with his back tensely arched, walks a few difficult steps on stiffened legs and then forgets the whole thing and returns to his normal business of mousing around.

The back flip is useful as an escape from hot pursuit. Executed at high speed it can carry a fugitive two feet in the air while the pursuer, unable to stop quickly, runs under him. The flipper makes a kind of Immelmann turn in the air, lands on his feet, and tears away on a reversed course.

Singer

Some observers mention a chittering sound that chipmunks utter and some of them have tried to render it echoically on paper with letters. This is chancey. A master flautist, unacquainted with the bird, would have trouble imitating the bobolink's song from the verbalizing of it in *Birds of America:* "Oh, *geezeler, geezeler, glipity, onkeler, oozeler, oo.*" We have heard nothing from Chippy that sounds like what the written symbols suggest to us but we have heard what we call, for ourselves, "singing." This starts with a quiet note pitched almost as high as Chippy's squeal but softly uttered. It trails off into a kind of purring. We hear it infrequently, but repeated by a chipmunk basking in the sun, it suggests complete contentment. Some think it is a love song, but who knows what it really means? It may parallel the kind of bitter profanity that men sometimes mutter through clenched teeth.

We hear another small sound that Chippy utters when he searches a human for a hidden peanut. It is audible only when he is within about six inches of an ear. It sounds like a rapid and continuous whispered imitation of his chucking but it may be nothing more than rapid breathing. Lungs so small demand frequent respirations.

Memory and manners

Chippy's memory is good, both for short runs and for long hauls. His precise repetition of circuitous unmarked routes has to be memory

first, before it can become habit. If there are more peanuts available than he can carry, he takes home a load and returns to the right spot for more. But that of course is what he would do with a hickory tree. Still, if he smells out nuts that are hidden, say, under a sweater, or in a pocket, he will take them away and return to look in the same place. Though he detects the scent that a nut leaves on the spot from which it has been removed, this is surely too faint even for *his* nose to lead him back into a sweater or pocket.

As soon as our more intimate chipmunk acquaintances get themselves moving in the spring, they give evidence of remembering patterns they followed last summer. Rhoda mounts a windowsill, puts her "hands" against the glass, and peers in; or, hearing movement on the second floor, she stands on the sill and gazes hopefully upward (and outward), waiting to pounce on a dropped nut. These are *her*

Stumpy, begging

patterns; no other chipmunk follows them. Stumpy, living under the steps outside the kitchen door, stands up on the top step and greets spring with his old pathetic look of imminent starvation.

You may ask how we know these are the same chipmunks. Obviously we don't recognize all of the individuals on the place. Thirty at least live within a hundred feet of the house and most of them are merely chipmunks, but we do know the half dozen or so that live within ten feet of the walls and a couple of others that make deliberate visits when handouts are available. Four of the lot have obvious marks resulting from accidents, but all of the "in" group have recognizable personal traits. Lucy for instance has no fur for half an inch on one side of her tail. This will be repaired when she grows her winter coat but she will still be recognizable as "Crabby Lucy." She isn't quite grown but she has her new burrow near the edge of the terrace and she has staked out one end of the paved area as hers. Since at least four other chipmunks, all larger than she, habitually come there for nuts, Lucy has her hands full defending her property. She can chase any one of them off, but not two at once. No one could mistake that aggressive personality, though it probably would not exist away from home.

MacTavish is a rough customer. Like all male chipmunks, he has less faith in humans than the females have, but after a couple of circlings (they're all great circlers) and backings away, he will rush up to a proffered peanut and snatch it from the fingers that hold it. He is so fast and so vigorous about it that we expect to be nipped severely by

32

mistake. Once he has his nut, MacTavish, nervous though he is, will forget all about the hand he fears, and sitting within an inch of it, will go through the ritual of proper pouching. The concentration needed for this seems to leave no room in his head for fear.

On the other hand, George (it should be Georgette) was born with gentle manners and a complete confidence in people. With only the slightest hesitation, she accepted the first nut that was ever offered to her. Most chipmunks shy from a hand that is suddenly reached down to offer a nut. Not George—she stands up to meet it and rests a cool paw on a finger for support. When she has pouched her nut, she looks

up for more and if more isn't immediately given, she climbs to a knee to investigate. Our neighbor, Lawrence, discovered recently that George will jump for a nut and hang on, swinging by her teeth, if he does not let go of it. George has still another caper that we have seen no other chipmunk perform; if the nut she has stood up to reach is moved a couple of inches horizontally, she will toddle after it on her hind feet.

Brains

Chippy's bright eyes, quick motions, and air of constant alertness make him look clever; but he is only "a participant in the general intelligence of nature." This is the kind with which birds build nests. Birds were raised in a laboratory for several generations with all nest-building materials deliberately kept from them. When, eventually, materials were given to a pair that had never seen a nest, and whose parents and grandparents had also been reared on foam rubber, they

unhesitatingly built to perfection the immemorial nest of their species.

Chip is born with enough brains to handle the normal problems of being a chipmunk, and also with a lot of information that he doesn't have to learn. He can provide himself with food, selecting only the kinds that are good for him. He can construct an elaborate dwelling, well planned for safety and warmth. He can escape from danger quickly, and hide from it cleverly—though a youngster once "hid" on a branch, a foot from a man, under a leaf that covered only his head. But any problem not included in the chipmunk book of instructions seems to baffle him. We hung a bird-feeding platform from the middle of a wire stretched between two trees. Chippy could smell the sunflower seeds on it and found that he could get them by jumping to the

34

platform from a nearby bush—a notable upward broad jump of nearly four feet. We pruned his bush radically. When he arrived next time, his hesitation showed that he knew something was wrong, but he couldn't figure out what had happened. Even when he jumped and fell short he didn't grasp the situation. He jumped short again and again before he exhausted himself and quit. The idea of reaching the seeds by way of a tree and the wire never got through to him. It got through to a gray squirrel at the first glance.

Nevertheless, John Burroughs watched a chipmunk extracting stones from his burrow. The stones had projections that made them slightly larger than the entrance. So Chippy grooved the sides of the hole at the right places to accept the projections. He pushed the stones through and then refilled the grooves with dirt. This looks more like a minor engineering feat than like mere instinct, but it is part of excavation and Chippy is thoroughly "programmed" for that.

We have read a report of some experiments to test the mentality of chipmunks. One of these required the chipmunks to find food in a many-branched maze, and then to find an escape door. It is remarkable that these expert maze builders, with supernoses, didn't all solve the problem at the first try. Even more remarkable, in the other direction, is the performance of one chipmunk on a different test. A nut was hung on one end of a long string that passed over a horizontal pole. The nut was too high for the chippy to get, but the long end of the string reached the ground. After a couple of fruitless jumps, this genius pulled on the string until he raised the nut and brought it over the pole, so that it fell where he could get it.

Sponging

From his own point of view, Chippy associates with humans only as a freeloader. His whole interest in people is the bonanza of food they offer him. To most of us he fully pays for what he gets with the entertainment he affords but he doesn't know that. Since it's true of other animals, it is probable that a chipmunk caught young and raised "by hand" will become a real pet, responding to affection. Adult chip-

35

munks that learn to suspend their fear of man to the extent that they will run all over him, risking capture or death, are concerned only with food, and remain wild animals in every way. Not even the friendliest of our chippies wants his fur stroked, or will endure it longer than an instant, and then only while he is intent upon something else.

Within this limit any chipmunk can be tamed by any person who will give the needed time and patience to the process. The amount of time varies with the sex and nature of the animal. Females are the easier to lure, and the few animals that are "born tame" are always females. There is one cardinal rule in enticing a chip: move as little as possible and make all necessary motions slow and deliberate. All chipmunks, however tame, are startled by quick actions and instinctively run away from them.

Curiosity and the aroma of nuts will bring any chipmunk to within ten feet of a seated person who is making no violent gestures or loud noises. Gently rattling peanut kernels in their shells is likely to bring one closer. For some reason, we also make kissing noises. These seem almost instinctive, but there is no proof that they affect the situation. Toss Chippy as many nuts as necessary, luring him a little closer each time by withholding the reward until you think he has reached the end of his courage. Give him two or three nuts at a time if he will wait around for them. To propel a peanut to where he can reach it, and still not startle him by the action of throwing it, restrain a finger with the thumb and suddenly release it to "plunk" the nut from the knee or from the arm of a chair. This is the same action as that which you might use to flick a beetle from your coat sleeve. Though fast, the gesture is so slight that Chippy doesn't see it.

All this sounds more elaborate than it really is. You will shortly have brought your quarry to the point where he will retrieve a nut lying at your feet. As soon as he does this, greet him with another nut held in your fingers, two inches from the ground or lower. A wary chipmunk seems to feel at a disadvantage if he has to take his front feet off the ground under such breathtaking circumstances. This is where you'll need your patience—and a back that can stay bent. Talk to him quietly. It doesn't really matter what you say; he understands neither English nor baby talk. And nothing is gained by pitching your voice high; after all, you are speaking to an adult. There is an unresolved argument around here as to whether a sophisticated chipmunk recognizes the word "peanut."

The nut in your hand presents a novel situation to your friend. He

needs time to overcome his timidity, but he always wants the nut, and because of that, you will eventually get him. Perhaps you'd rather not bother with all this? Quite a few nice people have no interest in close acquaintance with chipmunks, and it must be admitted that tame ones can be something of a nuisance. Except in the coldest and hottest weather, you never step out of doors without being panhandled. When Isabel feels neglected, she sometimes climbs the screen door.

Assuming you are willing to strain your back in order to gain the confidence of this fellow, and will wait for him, he will repeatedly creep near your hand, sniffing, only to back off, or run around in a circle. He will circle all the way around you and approach your hand from the rear, only to break off and circle around to the front again. He may, after a while, become interested in other things, or he may simply shrug his shoulders and go away. But he will come back, if not today, tomorrow; eventually he will creep up trembling to the nut and, jackass that you are, you will feel you have accomplished something.

Further training leads him to stand up to reach your hand, to climb (later jump) to the seat of a chair for a nut, then to your knee for a nut placed there or for one held in your hand. After that you'll have trouble keeping him out of your pocket, if that is where you keep supplies. Do not think that this is your personal pet. You have established his confidence, not just in you, but in all humans. He will now accept, and expect, presents from complete strangers.

Spunk water hole

Drinking

Many western ground squirrels, living in the desert, have adapted their bodies to conserve water. Since they also eat succulent plants that have themselves learned to store water, the squirrels need to drink only rarely. Eastern chipmunks can always get to water, so they drink it often. In winter they eat snow if there is any about when they come up to look around.

Chipmunks prefer to live on high hillsides, where in the nature of things water is not plentiful. Rain puddles dry up quickly, so, unless there is a high spring, the chips depend on "spunk water" that gathers in holes in trees and stumps. Even this evaporates in times of drought. When it does, they have to travel downhill far enough to find a spring or a stream. This problem doesn't arise for our chips, because the pool is easy to drink from and several bird baths are available. Even so, they often climb a gum tree near the house to drink from a spunk water hole thirty feet from the ground. Probably the water has a fine strong flavor.

As has been mentioned, chipmunks' mouths are hard to see from above. An observer has suggested that drinking chips do not lap water with their tongues but suck it up as a horse does. Aside from the fact that a chipmunk's mouth is ill-constructed for sucking, we think the evenly spaced rings of ripples that move outward when he drinks indicate that he does not suck. But we have positive evidence that chipmunks lap water. Just outside one of our windows a shallow dish

39

hangs, in an iron holder, on a tree. The water in it is intended for flying squirrels but birds and chipmunks drink it, too. Looked at from the living room, the dish is at about shoulder height. By stooping slightly, we can watch chipmunks at eye level lapping water with busy pink tongues.

Eating

Long lists of things a chipmunk eats have made dull reading for us and would be just as dull for you. He eats and stores all the kinds of nuts he can gather in the woods, with an apparent preference for those with thin shells. Hazelnuts, chinquapins, and beechnuts are cherished. Sometimes he buries nuts, as gray squirrels do, but whether this is because his storerooms are full or because he likes to have a few within easy reach, we don't know. As a rule black walnuts are too big for him to handle but he does store hard-shelled hickory nuts. One excavator found half a bushel of mixed hickory nuts and acorns in a burrow. By the way, frontier settlers used to dig up chipmunk burrows to get the nut stores from them.

hickory nuts   acorns   black walnut   hazelnuts

Since chips sleep most of the winter and hence can be assumed to eat far less than in summer, much of the large stores may serve to feed them in spring, when there is little other food available. It seems to be a fact of nature that nuts are normally plentiful in odd-numbered years and scarce in even-numbered ones. But sometimes the crop fails in a nut year because of drought or other disaster, and then the chipmunks have a hard time. Supposing they have stored enough in a fat, odd-numbered year to last through the expected lean one following (and also supposing such a store will keep that long), if the next scheduled good crop fails, they are thrown back entirely upon seeds, including what grain they can pilfer from farmers. Often these are not enough. Ernest Thompson Seton recorded that the failure of the 1907 nut crop reduced the large chipmunk population on his place in Connecticut to three individuals by the spring of 1908. Those three had survived by eating corn scattered on the ground for ducks.

Chipmunks always store a lot of seeds along with their nuts. If they

chinquapins   beechnuts   black gum berries and seeds   linden seeds

can get into a bird feeder, they will clean the thing out like small vacuum cleaners and emerge, not furtively, but with the look of sweet innocence on their distended faces. They store quantities of black gum seeds, often eating on the spot the purple-black pulp that surrounds them. They also take ragweed, broad-leaved plantain, and occasionally tulip poplar seeds. Almost any seeds that turn up accidentally will do, including those of watermelon and cantaloupe.

In summertime "the livin' is easy." Food is everywhere. Leaf buds and tender young leaves can be eaten. The corms of violet plants are a delicacy; so are pansy blossoms; and crocus bulbs, too, if individuals discover them. A chipmunk nearly cleaned us out of crocuses one summer.

Once in a while a chipmunk will break a small mushroom off its stem and eat all of it, holding it in his forepaws, biting off pieces as one would from an apple. More often he takes a bite or two in passing and leaves the rest of the mushroom standing. He eats both of the two

Puffball

kinds we recognize as edible—puffballs and the umbrella kind with pink gills that grows in the fields. The several other varieties he eats we are unable to identify, and are unwilling to test on his recommendation.

In addition to dogwood berries chipmunks find many other kinds from June through early fall: shadblow, wild cherry, wild grape

False solomon's seal

(sour!), ash berry, partridgeberry, and the scarlet fruit bunches of the false solomon's seal. These last grow at the end of a stalk, which their increasing weight bends lower and lower. The chipmunks don't wait for them to reach the ground—they jump for them.

They love all kinds of ripe fruit, wild or cultivated. Moldy blueberries and soft-sided strawberries tossed out of a kitchen window are eaten on the spot with obvious relish. They dote on tomatoes, especially the small "cocktail" kind, and on peaches, apples, and pears.

It seems likely that food is the real motive behind chipmunk curiosity; it leads them to explore the tops of outdoor furniture, the undersides of automobiles, and the insides of all penetrable enclosures. Once, the front door had to stand open until the freshly painted doorsill dried. We never saw the intruder, but we cleaned his gray paint tracks off the living-room floor.

There's a country story that says chipmunks are able to store ripe cherries in their burrows and keep them in edible condition. We have heard it told circumstantially: the cherries, with their stems bitten off, are ranged neatly side by side on dry grass! Don't believe a word of it. Chipmunks store nothing that isn't constructed by nature to keep well, except some seeds that occasionally sprout in storage and probably are eaten anyway.

Chippy also eats a lot of meat. He sometimes tries, and fails, to catch butterflies on the wing. He will stalk and pounce upon June bugs, grasshoppers, katydids, dragonflies, and cicadas (seventeen-year locusts). To see him eat a cicada without bothering to kill it first is a dreadful sight. He will not disdain an earthworm if he chances upon one, nor a bird's egg, nor for that matter a very young bird. But his depredations in this direction are not extensive enough to make him a menace. He is not a hunter of young birds; he merely finds one here and there. It's said that he sometimes does invade the nest of a white-footed mouse to get the young and eat them. He has even been known to eat young snakes.

There is an old trellis post here that has a deep cavity in it near its top. A pair of chickadees raised their family in it one summer and returned to it the following year to repeat the performance. But Henrietta, burrowing about, found that the hole ran all the way to the bottom of the post. She ascended it from underground and ate the eggs in the nest near the top. An uproar in the chickadee world led us to discover the crime—and the culprit, when Henrietta's placid face appeared framed in the opening.

The birds are well aware of Chippy's taste for eggs and nestlings and often operate on the assumption that the best defense is offense. Recently a chipmunk climbed a bush honeysuckle to get its succulent

44

red berries. He was already in trouble. A single branch was too limber to support him, so he was trying to climb two at once. There was no room in his mind for eggs; but a catbird, whose mate was nesting in a dense boxwood only six feet from Chippy, feared the worst. Squawking his harsh war whoop, he dive-bombed the intruder and knocked him clear out of the bush. Terrified, Chippy took cover—in the wrong place—under the boxwood. He came out again squealing, with the bird riding on his back.

Casual associates and enemies

Chippy gets on quite well with most other animals. When a robin lands near him, he will usually rush it. This results in nothing worse than the bird's rising a foot or so and landing again after the express has passed. It seems to be mere fun. Chippy has nothing against the bird. In fact, if the two find grain scattered on the ground they will attack it together peaceably, side by side. This applies to gray squirrels as well. If you would like to see a squirrel look burly, you should

watch him eating alongside a chipmunk. Chippy is also amiable to voles, the short-tailed, gray "meadow mice" that dig their burrows plumb in the middle of the space where seed is scattered for ground-feeding birds. A vole can pop-out-grab-a-seed-and-pop-back, with about the speed of a camera shutter. But when all is quiet in the early morning, or after sundown, they are more leisurely and they and the chipmunks feed together, taking no notice of one another beyond a little impolite pushing.

Vole

Red-tailed hawk

A large hawk will grab a chipmunk if he gets the chance, but Chippy is good at giving him few chances. A large owl, too, will catch a chipmunk if he can. He seldom can though, because he does most of his hunting at night when Chippy isn't around. Cats are bad, especially those that people, in their kind way, bring to the country to abandon. All cats are clever hunters, so most of these cast-offs manage to survive on birds, field mice, and chipmunks. Foxes can often catch chipmunks but blundering, noisy dogs can seldom manage it. Dogs waste an enormous amount of energy digging into burrows without getting within yards of the occupant, who perhaps watches the fun with his head out of his back door. Snakes, particularly blacksnakes,

are tough on chipmunks. They, too, can get into burrows, and though they cannot dig (never believe anyone who shows you a "snake hole" in the ground) they can go unerringly and silently to whatever is warm.

Like all mothers, a female chipmunk becomes desperately brave in the defense of her young. One of them held off a blacksnake, that was trying to enter her burrow, by repeatedly jumping on it and biting it behind its head. Her furious squeals brought help from us; without it she would probably have lost her battle. This does not mean that the snake was killed. Blacksnakes are valuable citizens: they eat rats and mice.

Chipmunks eat nuts, but weasels eat chipmunks and are probably Chippy's most dangerous enemy. Very long and very slender, a weasel can enter a burrow; worse, he can dig out a plugged tunnel. He is almost as good a digger as Chippy is. He can also climb trees. The preference of chipmunks for living in a high, dry locality may possibly be due to the preference of weasels for a low, damp one.

Weasel

Territories

There's no question that, just as Lucy does on the terrace, all chipmunks dominate small areas around the main entrances to their burrows. We are unfair to call Lucy "crabby"; she does only what all her kind do, and does it very well. Some observers have denied that chippies defend territories, but we have watched them at it many times and are very sure they do it.

The exact boundaries of these private reservations are almost impossible to discover, but all chipmunks know them. We can sometimes perceive one boundary or another by the behavior of the owner and his neighbors. Lucy, for instance, will pursue an invader down the path that leads to the garden, but she always abandons the chase at exactly the same spot. A line from that spot to her burrow would be twenty-five feet long. We don't know whether the point is beyond what she considers to be her actual boundary or not. Rhoda, at the front of the house, defends a far smaller territory. Three of her boundaries are obvious, though two of them, being walls of the house, need no defense. A third is the nearer edge of the path that leads from our front door to the lane. Rhoda's ancient stump, from which she jumps invaders, is only eight feet from the path and is approximately twice that from both house walls. Her perch is perhaps five feet from the edge of the lane, but we don't know how far her claim goes in that direction.

What has been well established in the case of birds and other territorial animals is evidently true of chipmunks, too. Chippy can dominate any other chipmunk invading his claim, regardless of size or sex, but his aggressiveness fades rapidly at the border. If the trespasser is (as is usual) the next-door neighbor, the situation reverses itself at the boundary. As soon as he crosses the line, the defender becomes an invader. The neighbor's courage then builds up at once, and he runs the erstwhile defender back home.

What complicates this further is an arrangement perfectly understood by chipmunks but confusing to humans. Trespass regulations are completely suspended for workers crossing a territory to get supplies from a distant source. Such a one, whether going empty to a nut tree or returning with bulging pouches, may cross a dozen territories unhindered, and hardly noticed, by their owners.

Burrows

Except for a general desire for concealment, it's hard to tell on what basis chipmunks locate the main entrances to their burrows. Many around here are well hidden in the dense evergreen periwinkle that covers the nearer parts of the woods floor. A good many are under bushes, or under woodpiles, or stonepiles. We often come upon an entrance covered with a large leaf, but we have never seen a chipmunk covering one, so the leaves may have blown there. One householder makes use of a tulip tree root. The tree is healthy, but this one

root is long dead and hollow. It makes an excellent tunnel. Some diggers put their front doorways in mown grass, simply sinking a vertical well. But one has sunk her well in the crushed stone of the lane within inches of the tracks of automobile tires; truck tires pass right over it. Sixty years ago Seton reported such a hole in his lane. For two summers he tried to fill it with gravel and for two summers the owner opened it up again after every filling—always taking the gravel from underneath, down into the burrow. A chipmunk never leaves trash around his entrance; holes in the grass are as clean as if they had been bored with an auger. Since the grass grows undisturbed right up to the edge, such holes are quite hard to see. The owners try to keep the grass looking normal; they enter by diving into the hole from several inches away.

At the surface, the bore of a chipmunk hole is exactly large enough for the owner to get through and not a fraction of an inch larger. An inch and a half is usually enough; sometimes the owner gets in only with a struggle and much kicking. When a foraging householder comes home with both pouches filled, he commonly has to unload at the entrance and let his burden fall in ahead of him—his filled cheek pouches are much too wide to let him pass through the opening.

The absence of any excavated dirt around most chipmunk holes has led to the weak joke that Chippy starts digging at the bottom and works upward. Actually he starts operations at the surface with a work hole that, in most cases, will never be used for anything else. This hole

may be twenty or thirty feet from the point where the main entrance will be opened. As dirt piles up around the work hole, Chippy commonly scatters it and covers it with leaves and litter. When he isn't using it, Chip plugs up the work hole from the inside. Sometimes no effort is made to hide dirt. Henrietta has her entrance in the grass of the garden terrace. Six feet away is the dry wall that holds back soil to keep the terrace level. A crevice halfway up the wall is Henrietta's work hole. She kicks dirt out of it and cares not where it goes from there. Every spring we uncover the flower bed below.

Normally Chippy kicks excavated dirt behind him, in a fixed reflex action: as soon as his front feet start to dig, his hind feet begin kicking. When Chippy has kicked up a pile of dirt in his burrow, he sometimes pushes it out with his nose. John Burroughs saw one shoving dirt out of his work hole this way. At least two observers found heaps of clay pellets, of just the right size, near work holes and have surmised from this that Chippy sometimes carries dirt in his pouches, but no one seems to have seen him actually doing it.

He excavates and moves an incredible amount of dirt. A work hole on our flagstone terrace yielded a full bucket of mealy clay on four consecutive summer days. Perhaps the digger knew we would haul it away; certainly he made no effort to hide it. Burroughs measured a pile alongside a newly plugged work hole and found that it amounted to a "plump bushel." From this, on the basis of his bulk as compared with that of a chipmunk, a man (working with hands and feet only, remember) should be able to dig something like a ten-foot cube of dirt. This comparison is worthless of course, since it disregards some important differences in the two animals.

The only way to examine the inside of a chipmunk burrow is to dig it out. This is not only hard labor, it also requires as much care as an archeological dig; it is trowel work, not spade work. We have never dug out a burrow but other people have. The earliest description of a burrow, by Peter Kalm in 1748, is a little sketchy. He said that chipmunk burrows "go deep and commonly further inwards divide into many branches." Mr. J. A. Panuska and Mr. N. J. Wade dug out a number of them around 1953 and what follows is largely based upon their thorough report.

The Panuska-Wade investigation found many small variations but were able to classify burrows as two main types: "simple" and "extensive." They found more than twice as many simple ones as extensive ones. Few of the simple ones went deeper than a foot or so, and none of them had sealed-off work holes. There was but one small living chamber, with one, or at most two, short tunnels leading to it. None of these simple burrows had separate storage rooms, and there was stored food in the living rooms of only two of them out of twenty-one that were examined. Black topsoil, tracked into the tunnels of all the simple burrows, showed that traffic was heavy in them. This might indicate that they served as "bomb shelters" for the whole chipmunk population. Perhaps they were bachelor quarters for males; but even these would need some storage space, though perhaps not in midsummer, when the investigating was done. A third likely possibility: they were the unfinished burrows of youngsters born in the spring of that year.

An extensive burrow is just that. Its lower levels reach as much as three feet below the surface, and two of its entrances may be as much as thirty feet apart. Obviously, Chippy is a born digger and loves his work. One of the earlier reports says that the observer has never seen a chipmunk digging and never knew anyone who had seen one dig. Certainly nobody ever saw a chipmunk digging underground, but Chippy constantly makes shallow holes to get grubs, or to bury food. His forefeet, working with alternate strokes, fairly fly and as dirt piles

53

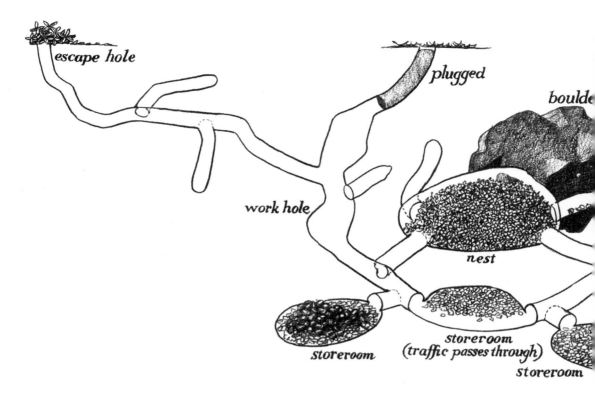

escape hole

plugged

boulde

work hole

nest

storeroom

storeroom
(traffic passes through)

storeroom

up behind him, he kicks it away with his hind feet. Compared with the large, clawed "shovels" of that other great digger, the mole, Chippy's "hands" seem too delicate for digging, but each of them is armed with four strong, curved claws; and it is the shoulder muscles that do the work after all.

There's little doubt that the extensive burrows are dug by and for females. They provide better protection for babies, which are born in them, and more storage space for food than the burrow of a lone male. Imagining ourselves shrunk to chipmunk size, and disregarding the fact that the tunnels, from a foot or so inside the entrances, are as dark as the inside of your hat, we will explore Isabel's burrow. Take it as a typical example; no two of the dens are exactly alike.

The entrance is a well, an inch and a half in diameter and eight inches deep, sunk in level ground. Considering your odd way of moving about, you will be allowed to enter feet first; Isabel goes in nose first. From your feet, at the bottom of the well, a tunnel slopes down-

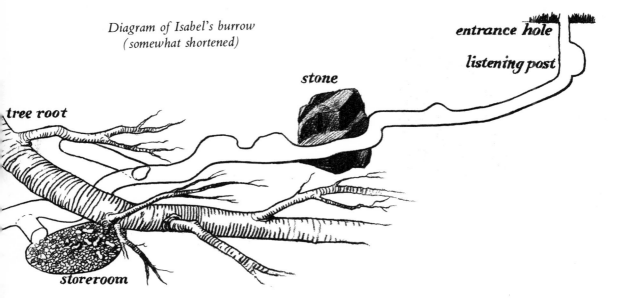

entrance *hole*

listening *post*

stone

tree root

storeroom

ward as steeply as a sliding board. You will notice two things as you start down: first, that the tunnel is twice as big as the narrow well; second, that there is a niche dug into the well that is just large enough for Isabel. This has been called a turning-around place but Isabel hardly needs that much extra space to turn; she can easily perform a somersault in the tunnel. More likely it is a listening post.

The tunnel levels off somewhat after a couple of feet and shortly we come to a kink in it. There is a big stone here and Isabel had to go around it. The passage is far from straight beyond the kink; it wavers this way and that, perhaps because the digger, keeping her general direction in mind, yet took the paths of least resistance. We pass through a couple of small "rooms" that seem to be only enlargements of the tunnel and to serve no obvious purpose. Beyond these is what appears to be a branch to the right. Explored, it dead-ends at six inches and may be guessed to be an abandoned experiment. Beyond it the tunnel dips down steeply and comes back up again. A glance at the roof reveals that we are ducking under a large root. When Isabel meets a root, she always tunnels under it, never over. It's been suggested that she may be afraid of breaking through to the surface of the ground.

55

Listening post

Actually we are now more than two feet below the surface and have traveled twenty-four feet from the bottom of the entrance well. An opening on the left just beyond the root admits us to a cavity about ten inches long with the bulging side of the tree root showing across one end. The room is about seven inches wide and its domed ceiling is five inches high. The floor is fairly level and is neatly carpeted with cut-up bits of dry leaves, each piece irregularly shaped and roughly half an inch each way in size. Scattered on the leaves are (surprise!) a few peanuts and a few empty shells.

Storeroom

Isabel uses quantities of dead leaves. She is never seen chopping them up, so it follows that she must do that underground, but she is frequently seen gathering them and it is an entertaining performance. She is particular about weather. A wet day won't do; the leaves would never dry out in the burrow. A very dry day won't do either. On such a day the leaves are too brittle to handle; they break. Isabel picks a day with just enough humidity to make them slightly limp. She uses many oak leaves, with no special preference as to the exact species of oak. You'd have to be a chipmunk to know the real reason for the selection; a human knows only that oak leaves are thickish and have a pleasant smell. Isabel selects big leaves. First she bites off the stem. Then, holding the stem end in her teeth, she stands upright and uses her forelegs as arms to fold both edges of the upper part of the leaf inward. This is quite a struggle. She can't fold the whole length of

Gathering leaves

the leaf at once, so as soon as she has mastered the first inch, she starts rolling the folded part downward. She uses her teeth and her neck for the job and holds the sides with her hands until the roll keeps them in place. The rolling moves the leaf upward and Isabel repeats her operations until it is a neat package held crosswise in her mouth. It's too long for the pouches. Finished, she always straightens up for a quick survey of her surroundings before she takes the leaf below. Thin gum leaves are wadded whole and pouched. Rhoda once spat one out to make room for a peanut.

Unless you'd like to stop and eat a slightly stale peanut, we can continue a little farther downward to the point where the passage really does branch. The left-hand fork still descends, past three more carpeted storerooms, one of them nearly filled with mixed seeds and nuts. Beyond the storerooms this passage climbs upward to rejoin the right-hand fork, which we will take. It starts up at once. A steep climb of ten inches brings us into a chamber much larger than the storerooms. Like those rooms, it is roughly oval but, being dug against a boulder, one wall is irregular. The ceiling is six inches high and a few small roots show in it. The invisible floor seems to be about fifteen inches long and a foot wide. The whole space is filled with chopped-up leaves that reach almost to the roof. This is Isabel's bed and her nursery. Here, rolled into a ball and buried in the leaf chips, she sleeps through the coldest part of the winter. She is warm enough in her insulated bed, well below the frozen part of the ground. The cold protects her from her enemies by freezing the plugs of dirt she puts in the entrances to the burrow. In this nest, her babies will be born, but we'll come back to them. Let's see the rest of the burrow now.

A couple of short dead-end passages start off from the back wall of the sleeping room, serving no known purpose, though there are a few empty acorn shells in one. It was long claimed that each chipmunk burrow had a chamber that served as a latrine but no investigation appears to have revealed one. Chipmunks are cleanly animals; caged, they will always go to the same corner to defecate, and there is evidence that something similar is done in the wild, but few feces have been found in burrows.

At the far end of the bedroom an exit connects with the storeroom passage, and a "hallway" just beyond the junction leads into the large work tunnel which rises quite steeply toward the surface. It is irregular in size and shape and is in general much larger than any of the other passageways. Its main part, about three feet long, is from four to ten inches wide; but the last foot, just below the surface, narrows to two inches, and most of it is plugged with dirt. Outside, the closed end is completely hidden by leaves under a clump of viburnum. Halfway up the work tunnel is the opening into the escape tunnel, or back door. This passage is about eight feet long and quite crooked, with two blind branches. Isabel has hidden its surface opening under the periwinkle.

The long sleep

In midsummer when the weather gets really hot, in the "dog days" of late July and August, our chipmunks nearly disappear. You may see an occasional individual in early morning, or, more rarely, after sundown. Through the heat of the day, they keep to their air conditioned dens. In these parts the temperature at the bottom of a deep burrow stays close to fifty degrees the year round. Some early writers suggested that this summer disappearance indicated migration, that most of the chipmunks had moved to a new neighborhood. But no one has seen chipmunks migrating, and our familiars show up two or three summers in succession, which is about as long as a chipmunk lives.

When the chippies appear again in September, they have lost all interest in peanuts—and hence in humans. The earth is yielding its bounty then and the serious business of gathering and storing it becomes a full-time chipmunk job. All through September, October, November, and even into December, the whole population hauls food in endlessly repeated trips: empty from burrow to source, and back loaded, until one would expect the pads of their feet to wear out.

They don't seem much affected by cold weather. Some diehards are still at it here as late as the middle of December even if there is some snow on the ground. Dr. Allen reported seeing the last chipmunk at her home in upper New York state on a snowy November twenty-ninth, with the noon temperature at twenty-two degrees.

When the last provisions are in and, with luck, all the larders are full, Chippy plugs the outer ends of all access tunnels. Ordinarily the plugs don't reach the surface. Peering into a hole, one can see the bulging tops of them two or three inches below ground level. Whether or not any interior plugs are used is a matter known only to chipmunks. Nor has Isabel reported on whether she fluffs up her bed before retiring. But retire she does. Deep in her chopped leaves she rolls herself into a ball like a hedgehog, brings her tail under her and on up over her nose—and sleeps. But this is no ordinary sleep; Isabel's whole body slips into a torpid state. Her breathing slows down and so does her normally rapid heart beat; her temperature drops almost to that of her surroundings. She needs little food or water. This is hibernation, but not quite such profound hibernation as that of a woodchuck, which is a completely immobile coma. If Isabel is disturbed she half wakens and moves a little, groggily. A woodchuck lives through the winter on food he gorged in the fall and stored in the form of fat. It seems certain that Isabel must wake from time to time and eat. If not, why all those filled pantries?

Years ago on a cold November evening, we found a chipmunk apparently dead. Incidentally, except for a couple that had met with obvious accidents, this is the only inert body of one of these fellows we ever came upon. This one, however, moved slightly when we picked him up, so we brought him indoors and made him comfortable in a box with wire cloth over its top. Warmth brought a return of vitality and within an hour our guest was cracking nuts with gusto. He spent the night and took off for home at a lively pace when released in the morning.

It can't be said with certainty that all chipmunks come out of their burrows in midwinter but many of them do. In the course of a few bright days at the end of January or the beginning of February some at least come up into the sunshine and actively chase one another over the snow. Then everybody goes back to sleep and no chipmunk is seen again until March.

Life span and death

A captive chipmunk is reported to have lived eight years. This is only mildly remarkable, since all captive animals tend to live longer than their wild brothers. We know positively that one free chippy lived four years at least, but the ordinary lifetime is probably three summers. A good many are certainly killed by other animals, though that has rarely happened where we could see it. We are convinced that most elderly chipmunks go into their regular hibernation and simply don't wake up. We can't prove this but there seems to be no evidence against it, and even if it isn't true, it's a cheerful thought. What is certainly true is that one after another of our old friends has simply failed to reappear in the spring.

Breeding and young

Up through the first years of this century, naturalists held the idea that chipmunks were socially inclined, and that pairs mated and lived together in the same burrow, as foxes do. Chippy's amiability suggested this and may have led these careful men to misinterpret what they saw. For instance, when John Burroughs saw chipmunk tracks in the March snow leaving one burrow and visiting two others, he took them as evidence of a social call to see how friends had made out over the winter. They were actually the footprints of a male whose instinct told him that the time had come to perform the duty of all male chipmunks—to visit the females in their burrows and impregnate them. A male may visit several burrows before he finds a welcome, and such occasions are the only times when a female will tolerate the company of an adult male.

Five days old

In our latitude these visits occur before the middle of March. Thirty-two days later, in April, the young are born. There may be from two to five in a litter. We have never seen more than four; three is most common. At birth they are a little larger than, but just

61

Fifteen days old

as naked and pink as, young mice. Their eyes stay closed for some days but this makes no difference—even after they open, they can see nothing in the stygian darkness of the burrow. The young suckle instinctively and grow fast. At five days old they are two inches long, plus three-quarters of an inch of tail. At fifteen days they have reached three inches and dark stripes are beginning to show in the short new hair on their backs; but their eyes are still closed.

A somewhat rhapsodic nature writer described young chippies racing and playing in the tunnels of the burrow. Quite possibly they do that, but how he could be so sure of it isn't clear. All we can assume is that they must do some moving around to develop their new muscles, since all other young things we know of do this. At a month, these are

Twenty-nine days old

obviously young chipmunks—almost six inches long to the tips of their tails, which are now covered with very short hair. Their eyes are open, though still small; their ears, too, are undersized. In another seven days or so these features will be almost up to normal, and the first small head will peer cautiously out at the sunlight from the burrow entrance. That first blast of light must be a severe shock.

In any litter of four, one seems always to be bolder than the rest, and one to be more timid than the rest. When the first three are out on the ground, examining anything and everything with avid curiosity, and the bold one is so far from the hole that his mother nips his bottom to chase him home, the timid one will still be sniffing the world tentatively with a nose barely above ground. Apparently one of the first

things Isabel teaches her offspring is her signal that warns of possible danger. Humans aren't told what it is, and can't hear it, but it can be given from some distance; and four kids get it at the same instant and make a concerted rush for the burrow. This usually produces a traffic jam at the opening, with a frantic youngster trying to wedge his nose in where two are already stuck.

For the week or so that the chiplings stay around the burrow, they cause humans to waste a lot of time watching them. Kittens are not more charming. There are constant chases and wrestling matches, but much of the play is preparation for the business of life. The kids stalk one another and pounce, and then roll over together with small squeals. Reasonably friendly nipping also produces squeals. Every now and then one, usually the farthest from the hole, will imagine an alarm and practice his speed at getting out of sight. Isabel doesn't seem to give them formal lessons, but she stops by frequently to sniff each one by way of counting heads. We have never seen her feed them, either by offering them food she has collected or by letting them nurse. She does seem to make a point of going through the grooming ritual where they can see her doing it, and they are prompt to imitate, sometimes with comical results. The balance of a small chipmunk isn't always sure enough to let him reach around to the base of his tail without upsetting.

The intense curiosity persists and the mousing around that they will do all their lives begins in the first week above ground. The examination of all phases of their surroundings is carried a little farther afield each day. They pick up some small thing and smell it. Mostly they drop it, but sometimes they eat it. Usually we don't know what they are eating; but one thing we have seen them eat is the immature green berries that the black gum trees drop in great quantities, because gum trees always start more berries than they can support. We have not seen the young chipmunks gnawing on anything hard, though they obviously have teeth and will shortly have to put them to work. So, too, with digging. They are going to spend their lives at it; it is a basic instinct—yet we've never seen a juvenile trying out his ability to do it. Perhaps we have never happened to be watching at the right time.

The youngsters continue to grow rapidly. Within a week they have lost most of their baby look and become small adults in appearance. This is chiefly a matter of bodies growing up to heads. Only their size and their earnest curiosity mark them as teen-agers. They seem to lose interest in one another as they diverge on exploring trips and unless they are deliberately marked in some way, we can no longer identify them. Some people believe they graduate from family life at the end of a week above ground, and face the world alone.

We don't know this is true; nor do we know it is not true. In human terms it seems incredible that, say, a fifteen-year-old should be expected to get his own food and build himself a house; but chipmunks are not humans. It's certain that each of these younglings will have to dig at least a simple burrow and stock it with food before snow flies. Perhaps it is to force them to postpone their major collecting until the nuts ripen (and hence will keep) that their cheek pouches appear to grow slowly. Lucy, who was obviously born this spring, had some sort of burrow by July and was carrying peanuts into it—one at a time. She tried to get small nuts (those with only one kernel in them) into her pouches, but there simply wasn't yet room for them.

About the end of June there is a second breeding season. It seems to take place in a single day, though we have nothing more than an impression to back this up. The first sign of it is a wave of excitement in the chipmunk world; everybody who isn't chasing someone is being

65

chased. Most of the chases begin on the ground but not all of them stay there; quite a few continue right on up into the tall trees. Most are males chasing other males in an effort to eliminate competition; such chases commonly end in furious fights.

The other chases are males pursuing females. Those that are not ready to mate escape easily. Those that are ready allow themselves to be caught and the couple engage in a session of attractive love play. Repeated sham chases of a few feet end as gentle sham fights in which the couple roll one another over on the ground while uttering low-pitched cooing sounds. The summer mating takes place entirely above ground.

The offspring of these later matings are born in the burrow in August and appear on the surface in late September, too late to dig and stock a burrow before winter. So, instead of being shunted out to face life at the age of six weeks, this litter spends the winter with the mother in her burrow. By fall, her children should be old enough to help in gathering the food they will eat through the winter, but it isn't established that they do so.

The birds that stay with us over the winter, the woodpeckers, the titmice, the nuthatches, the chickadees, the cardinals, the bobwhite quail, all turn out in all kinds of weather to feed—even in the midst of blizzards, when the deer huddle miserably in some hollow, and all the small animals hole up in their dens for a couple of days until the worst is over. Once it is, regardless of biting cold and banked snow, the gray squirrels come out in the sunshine to steal birdseed and to unerringly locate and dig up nuts they buried in the fall. The cottontails nibble at leaf buds on low bushes. At night the raccoons and the possums sally forth in quest of any food they can find—mice, garbage, suet hung up for the birds. The foxes stalk field mice, rabbits, quail, or, with great luck, hens. Even the flying squirrels glide to our shutters in small squadrons and crawl down them to a swept windowsill, for nuts. For all these, the margin of survival is narrow. Only the woodchucks and the chipmunks, safe, and profoundly asleep, can let winter take care of itself.

INDEX

ABOUT THE AUTHOR

Edwin Tunis, noted author and illustrator, was born in Cold Spring Harbor, New York. He now lives in Maryland, in a charming house in a wooded area where he has ample opportunity to observe chipmunks and other wildlife. His wife, who is an artist, shared the day-to-day observations that went into the creation of CHIPMUNKS ON THE DOORSTEP.

Mr. Tunis's special interest in American history has resulted in a distinguished group of books depicting in words and pictures many aspects of this country's past: *Shaw's Fortune, Colonial Craftsmen, Colonial Living, Frontier Living, Indians,* and *The Young United States: 1783 to 1830,* which was runner-up for the National Book Award in 1969. He has also written and illustrated *Oars, Sails and Steam,* a story of boats from the earliest days; *Wheels: A Pictorial History,* a record of man's greatest invention and the vehicles that developed from it; and *Weapons: A Pictorial History.* CHIPMUNKS ON THE DOORSTEP is his first book of natural history.